MIRIAM'S JOURNEY
Discovering A New World

By Robin K. Levinson
Gali Girls Jewish History Series

Published by Gali Girls Inc.
Copyright © 2006 by Gali Girls Inc.

Published by
Gali Girls Inc.
48 Cranford Place
Teaneck, NJ 07666

Please visit our website at www.galigirls.com

Library of Congress Cataloging-in-Publication Data

Levinson, Robin
Miriam's journey : discovering a new world / by Robin Levinson ;
illustrated by Drusilla Kehl
p. cm—Gali Girls Jewish History Series
Summary: Ten-year-old Miriam Bloom is excited to learn that she
and her family are leaving their shtetl in Russia to move to America;
but she could never predict the challenges her family would
encounter along their journey, and how Jewish values restore hope
and strength to her family.

ISBN 0-9773673-0-4

10 9 8 7 6 5 4 3 2 1

CONTENTS

Dedicated to my grandmother,
Maime Michaels, and to my daughter
Zoë Mae Levinson

דור לדור

THE BLOOM FAMILY

Miriam Bloom and her sisters had never seen their mother so excited.

"Guess what, girls!" Rose Bloom shouted, bursting through the door of their ramshackle house. She was out of breath with joyful tears splashing onto her round cheeks.

In Mama's right hand was Papa's latest letter, which had just arrived. In Mama's left hand were four blue cards, each with a drawing of a ship and words printed in a language Miriam recognized as English. Mama waved the cards in the air and triumphantly proclaimed: "We're finally going to America!"

"HOOORAAAY!" Miriam, Ida, and Sophie yelled, jumping like monkeys on the mattress they shared.

If not for their different heights, it would be hard to tell the sisters apart. All had their father's auburn hair and their mother's pale blue eyes. Their lips were red as cherry lollipops and curved into a natural smile—especially today.

At age 12, Ida was the oldest. She was an impatient, hardworking girl who eagerly took on the most challenging chores, like carrying water, washing clothes, and plucking feathers off a chicken for Shabbat dinner. This freed up Mama to spend more time doing the chores Papa used to do, like tending their vegetable garden and chopping wood.

The youngest sister was 5-year-old Sophie. Quiet and painfully shy, Sophie always hid behind her mother's skirt when introduced to someone. She loved to draw pictures of her family and her surroundings—and was quite good at it. Often, you could tell what kind of mood Sophie was in by looking at her drawings.

In the middle was Miriam, age 10, a tomboy who loved climbing trees and running through the overgrown field of grass outside her school. She admired her older sister, who seemed so grown up, especially since Papa left. At the same time, Miriam felt protective over her little sister. She'd make up games or sing silly songs to comfort Sophie when she was afraid.

Perhaps more than anything, Miriam loved to learn. For the past 12 months, she was learning to speak English. She'd obtained an English primer from her teacher and studied it with Mama. Every day, Miriam memorized a new phrase, such as "What's your name?" "Where is the post office?" or "Please pass the salt." Then she would teach what she learned to Ida and Sophie.

Miriam was so thrilled by the idea of moving to America that she leaped off the mattress and into her mother's arms, knocking them both to the dirt floor. Like playful kittens, Ida and Sophie piled on top. Everyone laughed until their faces hurt.

A whole year had gone by since the girls had seen their Papa, Samuel Bloom. He left Russia and sailed on a huge steamship across the Atlantic Ocean to America.

"There's no future for us in Grodek," Samuel told his daughters. Grodek was the name of their *shtetl*, or little village, near the shores of Russia's Black Sea. "I'm going to set up a business and find us a new home in America. As soon as I make enough money, I'll send for you. I promise."

Miriam desperately wished Papa could afford

4

to take everyone with him right away. But he barely scratched out a living mending and altering clothes. Although Papa worked hard, few people in Grodek earned enough money to buy new knickers, skirts, or coats on a regular basis. The Bloom sisters wore mostly hand-me-down dresses in drab colors like gray or olive green. It took Papa two years to save enough money to buy his own ticket to America.

Papa's letters overflowed with vivid descriptions of his new home. He lived in a lively section of New York City known as the Lower East Side. There were many tall buildings, some 10 stories high, with shops on the ground floor and apartments above. There were also four- and five-story tenement houses, where many Jewish families lived in close quarters.

New York City was exploding with new immigrants, including Jews escaping persecution in Russia and Eastern Europe. From stores or pushcarts, you could buy anything you needed on the Lower East Side—from fresh rye bread and

candy to furniture and furs. Newspapers and magazines written in English, Yiddish, Hebrew, or Russian were sold on almost every street corner.

No longer was Papa confined to sewing patches on knickers and replacing lost buttons. In New York, he was gaining a reputation for crafting beautiful clothing for women and girls. Papa's letters often included sketches of his latest designs and small swatches of fabric. In New York, there were plenty of people who could afford the skirts and dresses Papa made. Still, it took him many months to save enough money to buy those four blue cards—tickets for passage on a ship that would finally reunite his family.

In the meantime, Papa continued to write home two or three times a week. Back in Grodek, reading his letters aloud at the kitchen table was an event, not just for the Blooms, but for their friends and neighbors, too.

"In America, everyone gets a chance to be successful," one letter said. "The streets are paved with gold."

"Paved with gold?" Sophie asked. "How could that be?"

"It's just an expression that means America is a rich country," Mama explained. "People can make a better living there than they can here in Grodek. In America, you don't have to worry about having enough to eat. In a sense, America's streets are paved with golden opportunities, Sophie, not real gold."

In Grodek, the streets weren't paved at all. They were made of dirt, with deep troughs on either side to help prevent flooding when it rained. There were no cars or bicycles. People got around on foot or on rickety, horse-drawn carts.

The houses lining Grodek's streets were small wooden structures with thatched roofs. In some houses, the roof could be propped up on sunny days to air out the rooms. Water was fetched by the bucketful from nearby wells and streams. Mothers cooked over fireplaces or wood-burning stoves. Since there was no electricity, hurricane lamps and candles provided light. The fireplace radiated warmth but often lost the battle against the brutal Russian winters.

Members of the tight-knit shtetl communities spoke to one another in Yiddish, a language similar to German but written in the Hebrew alphabet. Outside the shtetls, the Jews spoke the language of the country they were in.

The majority of Jews in the shtetl were quite

poor when it came to money. But when it came to kindness, they were very rich. For example, each Jew felt an obligation to take care of the other, and Miriam was no exception to that rule. She tried to be a "good Jew" by treating others as she would like to be treated, just as the Torah teaches. She also tried to be generous, a value she learned from Papa. As Grodek's most sought-after tailor, he never charged his customers a penny more than they could afford. When necessary, he'd hem a skirt or let out a pair of trousers for free or in exchange for a dozen eggs or a bunch of carrots. The challenge was to make enough money during the week to buy some fresh fish or a chicken for Shabbat dinner.

Each shtetl operated like a big extended family. When there was a bar mitzvah, wedding, birth, or other special event in Grodek, everyone celebrated together, as they did with holidays such as Passover and Chanukah. Orphaned children, recent widows and widowers, and the sick were cared for by their neighbors.

On Friday mornings, Mama often baked a few extra challahs, which Miriam volunteered to deliver to some elderly neighbors. She enjoyed watching their faces brighten as they received the golden, sweet-smelling bread, still warm from the oven. Sometimes she would stay for a chat to relieve their loneliness or to learn about the past.

No one in Grodek thought twice about inviting a needy stranger or a yeshiva student to Shabbat dinner. People gave to charity, even when money was scarce, which was most of the time for many shtetl families.

Despite the daily struggles to survive in Grodek, the opportunity to make one's fortune in America was only a minor reason for Samuel Bloom to move his family there. The most urgent reason was to escape a life of fear. The year was 1914, and Russia was an increasingly dangerous place to be Jewish.

It wasn't always that way.

LIFE IN GRODEK

In the fifteenth century, Russia and parts of Eastern Europe were thought to be safe havens for Jews fleeing Spain to avoid persecution. In 1492—the same year Christopher Columbus set sail for India—Spain's King Ferdinand and Queen Isabella decreed that everyone in their country had to be Catholic. Some Jews decided to convert to Catholicism. But Jews who wanted to preserve their beliefs and traditions were threatened with execution, and so they were forced to run away.

Those who ran brought their Torahs and traditions to places like Poland, Germany, Hungary, Czechoslovakia, and Russia. At one time, Jews with "noble" professions, such as lawyers, wealthy merchants, or highly skilled craftsmen, were allowed to live in the big cities. But there were wars and rebellions, and when Russia suffered misfortune, the Jews were often blamed even though it wasn't their fault. Anti-Semitic regulations were imposed. The number of Jews permitted to attend high school and university was severely restricted. Russian Jews had to live in a region of the country called the Pale of Settlement. There, they established the shtetls, where they could practice their religion but were isolated from the larger Russian culture.

The living conditions in the shtetls improved only slightly over the generations, while the Jewish population grew steadily. By the time Miriam was born in 1903, Grodek was home to some 6,000 souls. There were cobblers, blacksmiths, artists, teachers, bankers, carpenters, midwives, and butchers trained to slaughter animals painlessly in accordance with Jewish law.

The children of Grodek attended primary religious school, or cheder, which ended in the fifth grade. Lessons focused on Jewish history, basic math, and Miriam's favorite subjects: reading and writing. After cheder, boys who wanted to be rabbis went to yeshiva to study Torah and Talmud. But most of the boys became apprentices so they could learn blacksmithing, tailoring, or another trade. It wasn't unusual for sons to work with their fathers.

After they finished fifth grade, the girls stayed home to look after younger siblings and help their mothers cook, clean, and run the household until they were old enough to start their own families.

Miriam was proud of Grodek's theater and its shul—the largest building in town. During the week, the shul served as a house of study, a place to meet, and a court to settle disputes. Every Shabbat morning, the shul brimmed with bearded men in black hats praying as they rocked and swayed their bodies, as if in a trance. After Shabbat lunch, the men would return to the synagogue to study that week's Torah portion and learn about various other Jewish topics. At the end of Shabbat, neighbors would get together to celebrate Havdalah, the end of holy time. Braided candles were lit then doused in a glass of wine, spices were sniffed, and songs were sung.

Miriam always looked forward to Thursdays— market day. People from shtetls throughout the area would gather in Grodek's central square to peddle their wares. Numerous carts and tables groaned under stacks of used books, seasonal vegetables, eggs, soap, shoes, candles, blankets, pots, and other items. Everywhere you looked there were people haggling over prices, chatting with friends, or lugging burlap sacks filled with newly purchased goods.

On one recent market day, Miriam tapped each of her sisters on the back and said, "Tag, you're both it!" Then she bolted into the crowd and found a hiding place behind a stack of wooden crates.

"We're coming to get you," yelled Ida, grabbing Sophie's hand. They searched high and low but couldn't spot Miriam through the noisy crowd.

But Miriam could see them through the cracks in the crates. She snickered quietly until she heard her mother's anxious cry. "Miriam, Ida, Sophie, get over here immediately!"

Skipping toward her mother, Miriam said, "Awww, come on, Mama. Please let us play. We'll be fine."

"Absolutely not," Mama snapped. Then she softened, hugged Miriam, and added, "I'm sorry, but those days are over, and you know why. So please stay close . . . I don't want to lose you."

Miriam understood that although Jews had lived in Russia for many generations, they were always treated as "outsiders." The rights Jews received depended on who was the czar at the time. Some czars were more tolerant than others. The current czar, Nicholas II, felt threatened by the growing Jewish population. He issued orders aimed at reducing their numbers to prevent Jews from becoming too powerful.

The Russian Jews, in turn, both feared and scorned the czar. Every so often, the czar would order a band of soldiers, known as Cossacks, to make life as miserable as possible in Grodek and the other shtetls. The Cossacks wore crisp uniforms, long black boots, and shiny swords called sabers. They galloped through the shtetls on horseback, calling the Jews names and yelling things like, "Get out of our country!"

Verbal assaults then became physical. The soldiers spat on the Jews and beat up whoever got in their way. They'd hurl rocks into windows, set fires, uproot gardens, break into the shul and slice up Torahs, and commit other acts of vandalism. Occasionally Jews were killed in these encounters, usually while trying to defend their families or property.

These vicious attacks, known as *pogroms*, typically occurred on a market day, which is why Mama insisted her daughters stay by her side. At the first sign of trouble, Mama and the other parents would grab their children and run home as fast as they could. They'd lock their doors and dive for cover under tables or hide in wardrobes. Anything left behind in the marketplace was smashed or stolen by the soldiers.

Russian police knew exactly what was happening in the shtetls. But they were under orders to ignore the violence, and so the Jews' pleas for protection went unanswered.

When a pogrom was over and things quieted down, the Jews emerged from hiding. Wounds were cleaned and broken bones set. Then a committee would form to inspect property damage and decide what needed to be fixed first.

Next, everyone set out to help one another repair their homes and businesses, clear away broken glass, and replant gardens. The cleanup could take weeks. Like the other older children, Ida and Miriam pitched in wherever they were needed. Even little Sophie helped sweep floors and rescue vegetables that the soldiers had scattered around the marketplace.

If anyone was killed during a pogrom, the rabbi made sure the body was washed and prepared for burial within 24 hours, as required by Jewish law. Every shtetl-dweller would attend the funeral, bring food to the victim's family, and mourn. Be it a beggar, craftsman, farmer, housewife, or scholar, each lost member of the shtetl community was treated with the same respect.

When Miriam's parents were growing up, Grodek was attacked a handful of times. Now, pogroms were carried out with increasing regularity every few months, and the level of destruction was worsening. The normally resilient Jews were finding it harder and harder to bounce back.

Pogroms didn't always occur on market day.

One night shortly after Papa left, Miriam was awakened by the sound of footsteps and deep Russian voices in her backyard. She raced to Mama's bed and huddled under her blanket. Miriam's heart pounded so hard she thought it might fly right out of her chest.

"Why won't the Cossacks leave us alone?" Miriam cried out. "We never did anything to them. Why do they hate Jews, anyway?" These were questions with no rational answers.

"Shhhhh," Mama whispered, placing her hand over Miriam's mouth. "We don't want the soldiers to hear us, *bubeleh*. It will only invite more trouble."

A few frightening moments later, the soldiers left. But Miriam could not fall back asleep.

The next morning, the clothes Mama and Ida had hung out to dry the day before lay in tatters on the muddy ground. Mama was doubly saddened since the dresses torn apart by the soldiers had been lovingly stitched together by Papa. If their neighbors hadn't given the Bloom sisters some clothes, the girls would have only their nightgowns to wear to school.

One by one, the residents of Grodek packed up their belongings and moved out. The first to leave was Miriam's Uncle Yossi, Papa's brother, who settled in New York City and later brought over his wife and five children. Miriam's best friend, Goldie, and her parents were next. They moved to Chicago. Miriam's teacher relocated to Palestine, where some of her relatives lived. Eventually, Grodek had more empty homes than occupied ones.

So when Papa announced he was moving to America, Miriam wasn't a bit surprised. "It won't be long before we can join him," she thought excitedly. Though she never imagined it would take a whole year.

CHAPTER THREE

JOURNEY TO AMERICA

When he first arrived in New York, Papa lived with Uncle Yossi, sleeping on the floor. At the time, the Lower East Side was home to the largest concentration of Jews in America. It was also the heart of the country's garment industry. Fashion houses and boutiques were springing up throughout the neighborhood.

A few weeks after moving in, Papa bumped into a fellow tailor he'd met in the synagogue. The tailor had just replaced his old sewing machine and offered it to Papa. Papa set it up in a corner of Yossi's apartment and spent the next couple of weeks collecting fabric remnants—*shmatas*—directly from the fashion houses or through dealers on the street. From these leftovers and discarded pieces, Papa created women's clothing of his own design.

At Uncle Yossi's urging, Papa showed some of

the clothes to Joseph Steinberg, the owner of
Steinberg's Clothing Store on Delancey Street.
Mr. Steinberg called Papa's designs "refreshingly
original." He especially admired their colorful
prints and lacy sleeves. Predicting his customers
would snap up the dresses, Mr. Steinberg bought
Papa's entire inventory, ordered more, and
advertised the collection in the newspaper.
Mr. Steinberg was a smart businessman. As he
predicted, practically every woman in New York
wanted to be seen in something Papa made.

Eventually, Papa's income got large enough to rent his own apartment. "It has two bedrooms, and in the kitchen there's an icebox to keep food cold and fresh," a recent letter said. In the shtetl, the only way to preserve food was to dry it or soak it in brine. To Miriam, storing food in an icebox seemed magical.

Before Miriam could see the magic with her own eyes, though, there was packing and organizing to be done in Grodek.

"I want each of you to pick one small thing to take with you to America," Mama told her daughters. "We have a long journey ahead and just one trunk, so we don't want to *shlep* too much."

Miriam chose her rubber ball so she could play catch and volleyball in America.

Ida packed her only book, a frayed volume of funny children's stories. Books were rare in the shtetls because of their high cost. But since the binding was broken and the pages so worn, the owner sold it to Ida for only two kopeks.

Sophie was torn between her sketchpad and teddy bear. Miriam persuaded Sophie to take her sketchpad since Papa could make her a new teddy bear in America.

Mama packed their small quantity of clothes,

shoes, blankets, sheets, pillows, and dishes. She also carefully packed a few keepsakes, including the carved wooden mezuzah from her front doorframe; the family's white linen tablecloth—a cherished heirloom used only on Shabbat; and a pair of silver candlesticks, a wedding gift from her mother.

Since the Blooms could not afford passports, Papa had hired an agent from the steamship company to obtain immigration documents for his wife and daughters. Dozens of neighbors, including some of the elderly widows Miriam delivered challah to, gathered outside the Bloom home to give them a warm sendoff. Grodek's banker handed Mama a map, a few rubles donated by his customers, and a list of people to call on for help as she and her daughters made their way across Europe to their departure point in Belgium. As the banker hoisted their trunk onto a wagon, the Blooms tearfully hugged their friends goodbye.

They walked for days on end, sneaking across borders and staying overnight in the homes of friendly peasants, in abandoned barns, or with people recommended by their banker. A few times, Mama and Ida cleaned a house or did other menial work in exchange for food and lodging. They spent most of their limited funds on a train ride when

they found one moving in the right direction. It was a risky, arduous journey, and on many nights the Bloom girls would collapse in a heap of exhaustion and fall asleep immediately, forgetting how hungry and thirsty they were.

Finally, almost two months after leaving the only home they ever knew, the Blooms reached Belgium, where their ship, the S.S. Lapland, as well as their immigration papers, were waiting.

The voyage itself would take a mere fifteen days—nothing compared to what they had just been through. But to Miriam and her sisters, it still felt like fifteen months.

There were several decks on the ship offering different levels of service. People with the most expensive tickets traveled on the upper deck, where they slept on feather beds in private, tastefully decorated rooms. These first-class voyagers enjoyed three lavish meals a day, artfully arranged on porcelain china. White-gloved waiters carrying silver trays served fresh fruit with pancakes for breakfast, sandwiches and soup for lunch; and beef, chicken, or fish with string beans and potatoes for dinner. The afternoon and evening meals ended with cakes and pastries washed down with fancy coffees and teas.

Those with second-class tickets also traveled comfortably but not as fancily. Service in third class was bare bones. The Blooms and others who had the least-expensive tickets traveled in steerage, located on the lowest deck. There were no beds or privacy there; passengers slept wherever they could find space to lay down on a blanket or coat. Responsible for supplying their own food, steerage passengers brought items that wouldn't spoil too quickly, such as bread, crackers, hard cheese, carrots and other sturdy vegetables, dried fish, dried fruit, water, and wine. It wasn't unusual to see people trading or sharing whatever they had.

The Blooms were among hundreds of Jewish immigrants sandwiched together in steerage. But despite the dank and dreary surroundings, the mood was upbeat. New friendships formed; promises to stay in touch were made. People with better knowledge of English taught those with less knowledge. Friends and family members who had died in pogroms were lovingly remembered.

The immigrants spoke excitedly—in Yiddish, Russian, and broken English—of their plans and their hopes for a better life in America. Shabbat aboard ship was celebrated with singing, dancing, and reciting the traditional Shabbat prayers. This time, they added a special prayer, called the *Shehechianu* (She-hech-ee-anu), which thanks God for bringing His people to this moment in time. Miriam was a bit startled when she heard Jews from faraway parts of Russia and Europe chanting the same exact Hebrew prayers she had heard in Grodek her entire life. She closed her eyes and could almost hear Papa singing the same melodies in New York. In that moment, she felt closer to him than she had in a very long time.

Miriam, Ida, and Sophie fought boredom on the ship by telling stories, singing, practicing their English, and imagining what their new school

would be like. At least once a day, they'd climb to the sun-soaked top deck to inhale some clear, salty air. Once, a kind white-haired lady wearing a glittering evening gown offered the girls some leftover cake, but they politely declined because they didn't think Mama would approve of them taking food from a stranger.

Halfway through the voyage, the ship was slapped by a vicious storm. The vessel tossed for hours on the churning waves. Almost everyone got seasick.

"At least we don't have to deal with those horrible Cossacks anymore," Miriam reminded her sisters when they complained about the rough ride. "And in just a few more days, we'll see Papa!"

On the last day of the trip, the captain called all the passengers to the top deck to witness their arrival in America. The sight of the Statue of Liberty took Miriam's breath away. She remembered Papa's description of the huge green lady, holding a torch and wearing a crown, rising out of the water.

"If she could talk, she'd say 'Welcome to one and all!'" Papa wrote in his last letter home.

TRAGEDY STRIKES

The ship docked at a place called Ellis Island, a few acres of land in the middle of New York Harbor. "Gateway to America," the island was called.

First- and second-class passengers moved through the gateway easily. Since they could afford the most expensive tickets, they were assumed to be healthy, legal immigrants or Americans returning from vacation in Europe. No such assumptions were made about the passengers from third class or steerage.

The Blooms disembarked and were absorbed into a sea of people clamoring to become U.S. citizens. Those from the S.S. Lapland's lower decks were directed to the end of a long line in the Great Hall of the main building on Ellis Island. Voices in various languages and accents bounced off the walls like a flurry of ping-pong balls.

"Where's Papa?" a frightened, trembling Sophie whined.

"Don't worry. He'll be here," Miriam reassured her.

The Blooms' line slowly snaked into the infirmary where doctors and nurses were examining each immigrant, looking for swollen glands, strange rashes, or other signs of sickness.

"People with a contagious disease aren't allowed into the country until their symptoms go away," Mama told the girls.

Immigrants with severe mental problems were sent back to their native country because it was feared they could never become self-sufficient, taxpaying citizens.

After passing their physical exams, Miriam and the rest of her family were sent to the other end of the Great Hall to stand in yet another long line. At the front of this line sat a uniformed immigration officer with a handlebar mustache. The officer asked each immigrant to produce a birth certificate, passport, visa, or other documents proving their identity and country of origin. As they stood in line, Mama and several other immigrants fumbled through their pockets and bags, gathering paperwork.

After reading his or her documents, the officer wrote each immigrant's name into a ledger. If the officer couldn't pronounce a foreign-sounding surname, he simply gave the family a new one: Konchalovsky became Klein; Larionov became Levy.

The officer also needed proof that the immigrants had a relative in America who could support them or an employer prepared to give them a job.

As they waited, Miriam and her sisters scanned the crowd for Papa. All around them, other family members were finding one another. One little boy running to greet his grandfather tripped over Miriam's foot. As she helped the child up, Miriam saw what looked like Papa's feet walking toward her. But when she glanced up, it was her Uncle Yossi.

"Uncle Yossi! Where's Papa?" Miriam asked.

"Thank goodness I found you," Uncle Yossi said, returning Miriam's embrace but avoiding her question. Then he held Mama's shoulders with both hands. "Rose, it's so good to see you—but I have terrible news," he whispered into her ear. "Samuel, my dear brother, died last week. He had a heart attack."

CHAPTER FIVE

STRANDED ON ELLIS ISLAND

At first, Mama froze. Then she screamed, "Oh no!" and released a cascade of tears.

"What is it, Mama?" Miriam probed. "What's wrong?"

Mama was crying too hard to answer.

"Children," Uncle Yossi said. "Your papa died."

The girls looked at each other in disbelief.

"I don't understand," Miriam said. "He was writing to us all the time. He couldn't wait to see us."

"He apparently had a heart problem that no one knew about," Uncle Yossi said. "Your Papa died quickly, sweetheart. There was no suffering."

The sisters grabbed each other's hands, as if to stop themselves from crumpling to the floor. As they started to cry, Mama embraced her daughters. Uncle Yossi threw his arms around his brother's entire family and hugged them tightly.

Seeing their grief on display, a group of adults and children the Blooms had befriended in steerage gathered around them, offering condolences. Spontaneously, ten men, including Uncle Yossi, formed a *minyan*. Together, they recited the *Kaddish*, a 2,000-year old prayer recited in memory of the dead.

Amid all this activity, the Blooms failed to notice that they had finally made it to the head of their line. The circle of friends opened to reveal three girls and their mother, all sobbing inconsolably.

"What is the problem here?" the officer boomed from behind his beat-up wooden desk. Mama was too distraught to speak, so Uncle Yossi stepped forward.

"Are you the head of this family?" the officer asked him.

"Yes, sir. I guess I am now," he replied.

"What do you mean by that? What is your name?"

"My name is Yossi Bloom. This is my sister-in-law, Rose, and her three daughters, Ida, Miriam, and Sophie. Their father, Samuel, passed away very unexpectedly only a week ago. His family was on the S.S. Lapland when it happened and just now found out."

"What a shame," the officer said sympathetically, "but I must ask you, Mr. Bloom, are you in a position to give them a place to live and provide for their needs?"

Uncle Yossi said that, of course, he would take care of them. But upon further questioning from the officer, he was forced to admit that squeezing four more people into his tiny apartment would be hard. The small salary he made as a fish seller barely supported his own family, much less his brother's.

Then the officer asked whether Mama had a job in America or enough savings to support her children. Uncle Yossi didn't say anything, but the answer was written on his face. Uncle Yossi knew that his brother had spent his last dollar on those S.S. Lapland tickets and that Papa's apartment was already rented to someone else. He also knew that Mama had no work experience or formal education to help her find a job.

After watching Uncle Yossi struggle silently, the officer finally turned to Mama and said, "I am truly sorry for your loss, Madame." Mama was so upset that she forgot what little English she knew and asked her brother-in-law to translate.

"Please tell her that under the law, I cannot let her into the United States," the officer told Yossi.

"Mrs. Bloom and her children must go back home on the next available ship, which is due to arrive in seven days. We will arrange for all four of them to be on board."

As Uncle Yossi interpreted, Mama grew too panic-stricken to speak in any language. So Miriam stepped up to the desk.

"Oh, please, sir. You *have* to let us stay," Miriam begged through her tears. "We cannot go back to Grodek. It is too dangerous there. And we have no place else to go."

"Unfortunately, I have no choice but to follow our rules," the officer said. "There are cots in the infirmary for you to sleep on until the ship comes for you. Now, please go back to the infirmary. Who's next?"

For the first time in her life, Miriam felt hopeless. Sophie, still crying over her father, was too young to fully grasp what was happening. Ida knew exactly what was happening, and she was furious.

"I cannot *believe* they won't let us in—after all this waiting!" Ida shouted in Yiddish, loudly enough for everyone around her to hear. "First, Papa dies," she continued, trying to fight back a flood of tears, "and now we are stopped from entering the country that was supposed to be our home." Peering at the officer through narrowed eyes, Ida braced herself and screamed in English: "Americans are worse than the czar!"

Mama was mortified. Ida's outburst had attracted the attention of all the immigrants within earshot, and they were outraged by the scene unfolding before them. Word of the Bloom family's plight spread rapidly through the Great Hall, until an angry buzz drowned out the Bloom family's heartbreaking cries.

"She sure has *chutzpeh*!" somebody said admiringly, obviously impressed by Ida's forcefulness.

Moments later, three police officers appeared to escort the grieving mother and daughters to the infirmary. A rabbi who was also immigrating stepped out of his line and followed them. The police ordered Uncle Yossi to leave Ellis Island.

Meanwhile, under a shade tree outside the Great Hall, the final group of first-class passengers from the S.S. Lapland was boarding a ferryboat to New York. One of them was the white-haired lady who had offered Miriam and her sisters some cake. She was looking forward to returning home after her long vacation in Amsterdam. Uncle Yossi jumped onto the ferry in the nick of time. He was disheveled, and his hands were trembling. Concerned, the lady asked him what was wrong. Unable to stop himself, Uncle Yossi blurted out the whole tragic turn of events.

"How devastating," exclaimed the lady, after hearing his story, "and how unfair." She thought silently for a moment, and then she got an idea.

"Mr. Bloom, my husband knows a reporter from the *Jewish Daily Forward*. Are you familiar

with that newspaper?" Yossi nodded, curious to hear what the concerned lady had to say.

"With your permission, I would like to have my husband tell the reporter what's going on with your brother's family. If the public takes an interest in the story, it might pressure the U.S. government to do something."

"Thank you, Mrs. . . er . . ."

"Mrs. Jasper," she said.

"Thank you so much, Mrs. Jasper," Uncle Yossi said. "I doubt Rose would mind. She's desperate for help, and there's nothing I can do for her."

The lady opened her purse and pulled out a piece of fancy stationery and a fountain pen. Uncle Yossi jotted down some notes about the situation and described where in the Great Hall the Blooms could be found. When the ink dried, the lady carefully folded the paper and tucked it back into her bag.

"I do hope everything works out for your family," she said.

CHAPTER
SIX

A HELPING HAND

Two days later, journalist David Belfer took the short ferry ride from Manhattan Island to Ellis Island. The best writer on the *Forward*'s reporting staff, Mr. Belfer was a dapper man in his early 30s. He wore black, horn-rimmed glasses, which gave him an air of intelligence. An official "PRESS" card issued by the New York City Police Department stuck out of his hat ribbon.

Mr. Belfer had been to Ellis Island many times before, gathering news from Europe and information on the latest wave of immigrants. The doctor in charge of the infirmary knew his work and trusted him. He directed the reporter to where the Blooms were waiting.

Mr. Belfer found Mama and Ida sitting *shivah* on their trunk, staring at the floor. Sophie was sleeping with her head on Mama's lap and her feet on Ida's. A sketchpad filled with Sophie's drawings of sad-looking faces and other disturbing images lay on the floor. Miriam was pacing. She'd been crying almost constantly since learning about Papa, and her eyes showed it.

"Mrs. Bloom? Please pardon the intrusion," Mr. Belfer said in Yiddish. "I heard about your *tsores* through a friend whose wife was on your ship. I would like to write an article about your situation for my employer, the *Forward*, a Yiddish newspaper."

Mama was skeptical. She had never met a newspaper reporter before and never heard of the *Forward*.

"Why would you want to write about us?" Mama asked. "Why would we want to share our problems with the rest of the world?"

Ida also had her doubts. "What if we get in trouble for speaking out?" she wondered. "In Russia, if you say something bad about the government, they arrest you and throw you in jail!"

"That doesn't happen here," Mr. Belfer said. "The United States has a Constitution that guarantees freedom of the press and freedom to express your opinions. You can't get in trouble for speaking or printing the truth."

"In fact," Mr. Belfer continued, "sometimes going public with a problem creates its own solution. I can't guarantee any good will come of this; all I can do is shine a light on you, so to speak."

"Please let him do this, Mama," Miriam begged. "We've lost everything. What harm can there be in letting him write about us?"

"She's right, Mama," Ida chimed in. "Let's tell everyone that the Statue of Liberty welcomes the tired and the poor—but only if they're rich enough to rent an apartment."

Mama had to agree. Mr. Belfer immediately started asking all sorts of questions about Papa, about the pogroms back in Grodek, and the Blooms' fast-fading dream of a new life in America.

"All my Samuel ever wanted was for us to feel safe and secure," Mama told Mr. Belfer, who wrote down her words into his notebook.

"What are your options?" Mr. Belfer asked.

"We have no options," Mama replied. "They're sending us back to Russia, and that's the end of it."

Mr. Belfer asked if Mama had a photograph of Papa to submit with his article. From her purse, Mama extracted a picture of her late husband. She kissed the picture and made Mr. Belfer promise to return it to Uncle Yossi since she had no mailing address at the moment.

Mr. Belfer studied the picture. Noticing the strong family resemblance, he looked intensely at Miriam, Ida, and Sophie then wrote something in his notebook. In his article, Mr. Belfer would say that the sisters' beauty shined, even through their tears.

By now, Sophie was awake, holding her sketchpad protectively against her chest.

"What interesting pictures," Mr. Belfer said. "May I see?"

Sophie nodded hesitantly.

"I like this one best. May I borrow it?"

Sophie nodded again, edging her way behind Mama and Ida.

Mr. Belfer asked each girl to describe how she felt. Miriam and Ida both said they missed their Papa very much and felt angry and scared.

"What about our shy young artist here?" Mr. Belfer asked Sophie, who promptly ducked behind Mama's skirt.

"Why won't she answer?" Mr. Belfer asked Miriam.

"She always gets quiet like that when she's afraid," Miriam explained. "She didn't talk for three days after the Cossacks messed up our back yard."

Mr. Belfer also interviewed the chief immigration official on Ellis Island, as well as Uncle Yossi in New York. The officials quoted immigration law. Uncle Yossi described the challenging but generally happy life he and Samuel shared in Grodek when the pogroms were less frequent.

"How did Samuel feel after mailing off the tickets to his wife and children?" Mr. Belfer wanted to know.

"He was on top of the world," Yossi said. "It was the proudest, most gratifying moment in my brother's life. He spent his last days thanking God for his good fortune."

Back in New York, Mr. Belfer went to the store that had popularized Papa's line of clothing and requested an interview with the owner.

"Such a talented tailor and devoted family man, Mr. Bloom was," Mr. Steinberg told the reporter. "He worked so hard to bring his wife and children here. He made more clothes in a week than two tailors could make in a month."

As they spoke, one of Mr. Steinberg's best customers strolled by in a bright, paisley dress. "It's a Bloom original," Mr. Steinberg whispered to Mr. Belfer.

"Lovely dress, Ma'am," Mr. Belfer said.

"Thank you, sir. It's the envy of all my friends."

"May I quote you?"

Back on Ellis Island, a photographer from the *Daily Forward* arrived to snap some pictures of the Blooms, who were sitting glumly on their tiny cots. The rabbi was still there, comforting them and saying prayers.

Two days later, the newspaper published the photos—along with Mama's picture of Papa and

Ida's drawing of a sinking ship. Surrounding the pictures was a long article by David Belfer under the headline:

"SUDDENLY HOMELESS, FAMILY'S FUTURE WITHERS BEFORE THEIR EYES"

The report took up the entire front page.

—

A GLIMMER
OF HOPE

Among the thousands of people who read the story was Alan Rosen, a lawyer for the Hebrew Immigrant Aid Society, an organization founded in 1881 to help Jewish refugees settle in America. Ten years before the Blooms arrived, Mr. Rosen's family was helped by the Society, and he personally had helped hundreds of Russian Jews gain citizenship. But he never had a client with such bad luck as the Blooms. Mr. Rosen knew it would be difficult to fight the government's decision to send the Blooms back to Russia. But that didn't stop him from wanting to try.

The lawyer rented a small boat to Ellis Island. Because Mr. Belfer's article was so detailed, he knew exactly where to find Mama—at the east end of the infirmary.

"Good day, Mrs. Bloom," Mr. Rosen said in Yiddish, with a sympathetic smile. "I'm Alan Rosen, an immigration lawyer. I read about your situation in the newspaper. I'd like to try to help you if I can."

"Thank you Mr. Rosen, but I don't think there's enough time. In only five days, we'll be forced back to Russia," lamented Mama.

"I could file an emergency motion to bring your case to a court of law," Mr. Rosen said. "I could argue before a judge that your lives would be in danger if you are sent back. I'd promise that the Hebrew Immigrant Aid Society would help you find an apartment if you were allowed to stay here. I could point out that you are a healthy, able-bodied woman with a variety of domestic skills—you can cook, clean, bake challah, wash clothes. You could apply for work in a restaurant or boarding house. I could also investigate whether Mr. Steinberg owes you money for the clothes he bought from your late husband."

"Do you think any of that would make a difference?" Mama asked.

"If the judge is willing to consider all the facts of your case, he might reverse the immigration department's decision. That would give you and your daughters a chance to become American citizens, after all."

"Thank you for your lovely offer, Mr. Rosen," Mama said. "But we have almost no money to pay you, and this sounds like something that will require a lot of time on your part."

"Mrs. Bloom," Mr. Rosen said kindly. "I can't promise that I'll win your case. To be honest, the odds are not in your favor. Should I lose, you won't owe me a dime. But if I win, I'll charge you $100, which you can pay out over time."

Overwhelmed by his generosity, Mama was speechless.

"Oh, Mama, you have to give this a chance," Miriam pleaded. "For Papa's sake."

Mama looked deeply into each of her daughters' eyes and smiled. Then she beamed her smile toward Mr. Rosen and said, "Yes."

The lawyer grabbed Mama's hands and shook them vigorously. "Thank you," he said before rushing off to the courthouse.

Two weeks later, a follow-up article by reporter David Belfer appeared on the front page of the *Jewish Daily Forward*:

BRIGHTER FUTURE BLOOMS FOR IMMIGRANT WIDOW AND DAUGHTERS

By David Belfer, Staff Writer

NEW YORK CITY (July 22, 1914)—A New York judge has ruled that a Jewish mother and her three daughters who were about to be sent back to Russia may legally immigrate to America, despite the untimely death of her husband and no immediate means of support.

Mrs. Rose Bloom and her children, Ida, 12, Miriam, 10, and Sophie, 5, were finally processed through Ellis Island three weeks ago after six days in limbo. Mrs. Bloom's husband, Samuel, was a well-known and talented tailor who immigrated to the United States last year. He ran a successful clothing-design business on the Lower East Side before saving enough money to bring his family over. Tragically, Mr. Bloom died of a heart ailment while his family was on the S.S. Lapland en route to join him. He was 40 years old.

Because no one in America was able to take care of the suddenly homeless widow and her daughters, the immigration authorities had no choice but to turn them away. The Blooms were to sail back to the Old Country on a ship that left Ellis Island two weeks ago. But to their surprise and delight, the Blooms were not on that ship. Instead, they were already moving into an apartment in the city—with the help of the Hebrew Immigrant Aid Society (HIAS).

The bulk of the credit goes to Alan Rosen, attorney-at-law. After reading a story about the family's problem in this newspaper several weeks ago, Mr. Rosen took the Blooms' case to Judge Arthur Smyth. Mr. Rosen said he was lucky to have the case assigned to Judge Smyth, who is known for his compassion toward immigrants. Because of the

50

urgency of the situation, the attorney had filed an emergency motion so the case would be heard without delay. After an hour-long hearing, Judge Smyth declared the Blooms official refugees, which guarantees them save haven in the United States.

After winning the case, the HIAS rallied the local Jewish community, which donated money, furniture, clothes, food, and elbow grease to help the Blooms find and furnish an apartment and enroll the girls in public school. A schoolteacher from the neighborhood generously offered to help the family improve their English.

Joseph Steinberg, owner of Steinberg's Clothing Store, discovered Mr. Bloom's talent soon after he arrived from Russia. Mr. Steinberg had an exclusive agreement to sell Mr. Bloom's line of women's and girls' clothes.

Steinberg paid for Mr. Bloom's funeral, which was held the day after he died. Since Mr. Bloom's family was en route to Ellis Island at the time, Rabbi Joseph Levi of the Eldridge Street Synagogue led a special memorial service this week. Hundreds of Lower East Side residents attended, along with Mr. Bloom's widow and daughters.

"I am deeply moved," Mrs. Bloom said after the service when asked what she thought of the turnout.

Mr. Steinberg ordered a memorial plaque for Mr. Bloom and told his widow it would be displayed in the store. Along with Mr. Bloom's name, a picture of one of his designer dresses would be etched into the plaque.

Mr. Steinberg's kindness didn't stop there. After the memorial service, he offered Mrs. Bloom a job in his store.

"Mrs. Bloom's English is still shaky, so the Yiddish-speaking customers, I send them to her," Mr. Steinberg said. "She is a natural saleswoman. I saved a few of the dresses I bought from Mr. Bloom in the back. Showing these dresses to customers helps Mrs. Bloom keep her husband's memory alive."

Said Mrs. Bloom: "I am

so grateful to everyone in New York who helped us, especially the Hebrew Immigrant Aid Society and Mr. Steinberg. Because he took a chance on me, I'll be able to pay back Mr. Rosen for his legal services."

Miriam Bloom, the energetic middle child, said the only thing she expected to miss about her shtetl, Grodek, was how everyone took care of one another. Then she found out that along with their candlesticks and shoes, Jews bring their values and sense of community with them wherever they go.

"I imagined America as a big place where everyone just minded their own business," Miriam said, her blue eyes sparkling. "Then I get here, and almost everyone we meet wants to help us. When I grow up, I'm going to help people, too. It's what my Papa would have wanted."

THE END

GLOSSARY

Bubeleh: Term of endearment

Chutzpeh: Guts, gall, nerve, brazenness

Cossack: A soldier in the Russian army

Czar: Russian emperor, highest authority

Kopek: Currency, roughly equivalent to 1 cent in Russia (100 kopeks = 1 ruble)

Mezuzah: A small parchment scroll, usually in a decorative container, containing hand-written passages from the Torah. Affixed to the post of the front door and the entryway to each living space in the house, the mezuzah is a reminder that you are in a Jewish household that adheres to a certain set of beliefs and rituals

Minyan: Hebrew prayer group consisting of at least 10 Jewish men

Pogrom: A government-backed campaign of attacks against an ethnic or religious group

Shlep: Carry, drag, haul—especially things that are unneeded

Shtetl: Small Jewish village or townlet

Tsores: Trouble

Reyna Li is a 12-year-old Jewish girl living in
Kaifeng, China in the year 1175.

REYNA AND THE JADE STAR

On Reyna's seventh birthday, her father
handed her a gift—an intricately designed Star of
David pendant carved from emerald-green jade,
about 3 inches in diameter and a half-inch thick. A
dozen glistening garnets as big as pomegranate
seeds were embedded in the jade.

A six-pointed star means different things to
different cultures. To the Chinese, it symbolizes
hope that things go smoothly. "For the Israelites, it
means God is the ruler of the universe, protecting
us from all six directions: north, south, east, west,
up, and down," Yehuda told his little girl as he
handed her the star. He continued to explain its
significance.

"We call it a *Magen David*, or shield of King
David, and the garnets represent the 12 tribes of
Israel. Legend claims that Noah hung a large
garnet in his ark for illumination. Garnet is also

said to be one of the 12 gems in the breastplate worn by Moses' brother, Aaron.

"In our family, Reyna, your jade star has extra-special meaning because it has been handed down from generation to generation, just like our religion. Now the star is yours. Someday, I hope you will give it to your firstborn when he or she turns 7."

Chirping with delight, Reyna said, "Thank you, Mother," which was a strange thing to say since her mother had died right after Reyna was born.

"How could you know this pendant was your mother's? I never told you that husbands gave it to their wives," asked Yehuda, astonished.

"I knew because there were tears in your eyes, and right before you gave it to me, you glanced at the picture of Mother—the one you drew last year when I asked what she looked like," Reyna said. "So I figured that this star used to be hers."

"You're absolutely right, Cookie Nose. My grandfather gave it to my father when he turned 7, who gave it to me when I was that age," Yehuda said. "After your mother converted to the Israelite religion and we got married, I gave the star to her—to honor her conversion. She adored it and wore it everywhere. When Mother was carrying you in her belly, she decided she'd give you the star when you turned seven."

"Why seven?" asked the always-inquisitive Reyna.

"Seven is an important number for the Israelites because it's associated with Shabbat. The Torah says that God created the world in six days and rested on the seventh. Your mother loved to celebrate Shabbat, the day of rest. When I handed you the star, I was wishing with all my heart that she were here to give it to you. I guess that's why I got teary-eyed."

So exquisite was the jade star, it could bring tears to anyone's eyes. It was almost unheard of to see garnets or any gemstone embedded in jade since jade is so lovely by itself. It was also rare to see jade in such a vivid shade of green. Common jade was light green, dull green, or gray. Reyna's jade star was priceless, and that didn't begin to describe its sentimental value.

Reyna asked, "Who made it?"

"We believe it was made by one of the first Israelites to settle in China, at least 450 years ago," said Yehuda. "Our ancestors cherished this star. It has been in our family for as long as anyone can remember."

"Where did our ancestors come from?"

"After we were expelled from our homeland, Israelites attempted to spread out all over the world, but most countries didn't want them," said Yehuda. He went on to explain how a few brave and desperate Israelite families caravanned from Persia and other Middle Eastern countries through Central Asia. Riding on camelback, they crossed treacherous mountains, deserts, and wastelands until they reached the Middle Kingdom, which is what China used to be called around 718 C.E. The Israelites were traders of multicolored cotton fabric, which the Chinese had never seen before. Not only were the Israelites allowed to live in China, they were embraced by the ruling family.

For about 250 years, Israelites lived in small communities that dotted the Chinese landscape. Then, in 960 C.E., the emperor gathered together some 500 of these families and resettled them Kaifeng, a prosperous city and one of the "six great capitals of China." Encouraged to continue their customs and traditions, the Israelites flourished in their new home.

"Our ancestors who made it to China were very lucky," Yehuda pointed out. "Of the 12 original tribes of Israel, 10 have been lost in the fog of history."

The Israelites of Kaifeng were close to being lost, too. Some intermarried and raised their children as Buddhists or in other religions. Those Israelites who strove to maintain their heritage struggled because they had no central place to pray and study together. Over the years, with no focal point to keep their community together, their awareness of God's covenant with Israel began to fade. Alarmed, Reyna's grandfather, along with members of 70 other Israelite families, decided to build Kaifeng's first synagogue in 1163 to help them preserve their religious identity. Each and every Israelite in Kaifeng donated money, labor, or both to make it a reality.

The Moses Synagogue's design reflected the people who prayed and studied there. From the outside, it looked like a typical Chinese building, with its gracefully curved pagoda-style roof, courtyard, arches, pavilions, and great halls. Yet, the heart of the synagogue—its sanctuary where two sacred Torah scrolls were housed—was undeniably Israelite. It faced west toward Jerusalem and featured a large menorah, one of the oldest symbols of the Israelite people.

The first Israelites who moved to China were Caucasian. Over the years, though, many of them intermarried with native Chinese, and their children began to inherit dark almond-shaped eyes and straight, jet-black hair until the Israelites were indistinguishable from other Chinese. Even Yehuda's surname, Li, was Chinese; his ancestors had adopted Li because their original name, ben Eliezer, was too difficult for their Chinese neighbors to pronounce. Beneath their name and outward appearance, however—in their hearts, minds, and memories—Yehuda and Reyna were undeniably Israelite and deeply committed to keeping their heritage alive.

"Our synagogue renews our hope that you and the other Israelite children will teach our traditions to your children," Yehuda told his daughter on her seventh birthday. "Our family has some extra traditions, Reyna. Your name, which means 'queen,' was popular among Israelites in Persia, where our ancestors once lived. Passing the jade star to each new generation is another way we honor our family's heritage."

The star was the best birthday present Reyna could imagine. She carefully felt its smooth and raised edges with her fingers, and then she gave the star a little kiss. It felt cool on her lips. She held it to her chest, and the pendant quickly warmed to her body temperature. Then Reyna placed it gently on the table, beside the sketch of her mother. Two minutes later, Reyna picked up the jade star again. She was surprised to find it was still warm. This stirred Reyna's imagination. She decided that as long as the star remained warm, it would allow her to speak to her mother. She knew it would be just pretend, but still, she couldn't wait to take the star to her Thinking Place. She ached to tell her mother how much she wished she could have known her. She wanted to tell her mother what it's like to be Reyna, an only child who lived in the largest Israelite community in East Asia in 1175 C.E.

Jewish fun, Jewish pride, Jewish heritage

Gali Girls are the first Jewish dolls of their kind, offering young Jewish girls an opportunity to incorporate positive values into their doll play.

Gali Girls represent positive Jewish values such as kindness, respect, charity, and honesty. Gali Girl accessories create a connection between the contemporary Jewish girl and her heritage.

Each Gali Girl comes with a Hebrew/English name birth certificate, matching Magen-David bracelets, and a 10-piece wooden toy Shabbat Kit.

For more information about Gali Girls, or to order a doll, please visit us at www.galigirls.com, or call 201-862-1989

ABOUT THE AUTHOR

Robin K. Levinson has been a professional journalist since graduating from the University of New Mexico in 1981. Ms. Levinson began her career as a newspaper reporter and became a freelance writer and editor in 1993. She coauthored seven consumer-health books before shifting her concentration to Judaic topics several years ago. She is a regular contributor to *Jewish Woman Magazine* and a reviewer for *Jewish Book World*. She has won more than 30 statewide and national writing awards, including two Rockower Awards from the American Jewish Press Association. The Gali Girls series marks her debut in children's fiction. She lives in Hamilton, N.J., with her husband, Larry, and children, Zoe and Aaron.

ABOUT THE ILLUSTRATOR

Drusilla Kehl is a professional illustrator working in the advertising field. She graduated with honors from Connecticut College and has traveled extensively in Africa, the Middle East and Europe. Among her many interests are history and archaeology, academic art, and animal rights. She lives in New York City with her husband, a large cat, and many pet rats.